I0571075

CIRCLING: 1978-1987

CIRCLING: 1978-1987

DEJAN STOJANOVIĆ

Translated by the Author

New Avenue Books

CIRCLING: 1978-1987
English translation Copyright © 2012 Dejan Stojanović

CIRCLING: 1978-1987 is the English translation of the poetry collection *Krugovanje: 1978-1987*, originally written in Serbian and published in 1993, 1988, and 2000 (Belgrade: *Narodna knjiga*).

All rights reserved. Printed in the United States of America.
No part of this book may be used or reproduced in any form without written permission from the publisher, except in the case of brief quotations embodied in critical articles and reviews.

New Avenue Books

First Edition in English

Library of Congress Control Number: 2024951033

ISBN-13: 979-8-9919466-8-1

POETIC CIRCLES OF DEJAN STOJANOVIĆ

In a colorful landscape of contemporary Serbian poetry, a careful reader can recognize that one of its branches, with a decidedly reflective experience of the poetic tradition and heritage, corresponds with a Serbian medieval age, opens up for its Byzantine chords, and, in the context of contemporary poetry, is closest to Modern Classicism. In the first wave of Serbian post-World War II poetry, this stream was at the foundation of a revival, which is almost suppressed today.

It seems that today, in the atmosphere of almost complete saturation by the practice of ever-changing poetic trends, Serbian poetry is returning to its basics. This picture of a slow rebound, a long-awaited reorientation on the Serbian poetic scene, is already happening, by all accounts, and is sensed in the actual literary production.

Reading the book *Circling* triggers the associations of this wave, which is not underground anymore but has transformed into a poetic phenomenon. Dejan Stojanović is not influenced by any contemporary poetic school or fashionable poetic trend and is not trapped by some sensibility as a "follower." Stojanović, as a reflective poet of mature thought and discourse, revives the atmosphere of the ancient times even in the first layers of his poems. It is easy to notice what specifically marks Stojanović in Serbian contemporary poetry: In weaving his poems and building his lines, a poet has returned to the antique form of utterance, to the complex and slow movement of the poetic matter, to the dignified and solemn tone, and that kind of wisdom which was nourished in ancient times.

Far from experiments, challenges of hazards, and poetic adventures, Stojanović's poems exude the dignity of ancient forms. Like painters' techniques, Stojanović condenses his utterances into short, harmonious poems, most often colored with Mediterranean colors, surprisingly successfully. His poems, almost by a rule, are condensed forms of short utterances. In the book's second part, the poetic palette becomes darker with an introduction of fantastic and hallucinogenic elements and even apocalyptic tones. Nevertheless, the principle of condensation and consistency of form is never questioned. Apocalyptic scenes and images of evil are expressed in huge blocks that give the impression of the work of an architect or a sculptor. Such are the poems "Vision," The Chessboard," "Arrival of Darkness," and "River of Death," which all appear as compositions. There is a feeling that Stojanović wrote his poems along with visual compositions; to that extent, visual-imaginative effects are impressive.

Specific, surprisingly original, outside the collectively nurtured sensibilities and fashionable trends, Stojanović is an extraordinary example of creative individualism in a generation that nourished such individualism the least. For that reason, the book *Circling* is not only an example of an extraordinary poetic achievement, which represents a strong encouragement to the important branch of Serbian poetry, but is also an announcement of a moral and spiritual project. This project belongs to the tradition of Serbian poetry and thought in the best sense of the word.

– Alek Vukadinović
Afterword to the first Serbian edition (1993)

Contents

RECIRCLING

IF I AM

If I knew
That grass broods while growing

If I knew
That a bird longs for life while flying

If I watched insects
As they mate and chirp
I would have thought about meaning

If I watched waves and saw
How persistently they hit the shore

If I felt the call of earth by seed
All for all, life for life

If I watched the heavenly bodies
How each longs for a circle of fulfillment
I found soul in everything

I found traces of natural wisdom
In the slightest breeze and a bright smile
In cataclysms and changes

And although personal calling I sense
Who am I? Even if I am
I don't know

HEARING FAR

Mystery of knowledge once dreamed,
A spark of tightened vision emerges:
Cities, omens, squares, castles,
A landscape into a landscape merges to
Molded fugue—the line of Being

Vista replaces vista
Pulse trembles—secret membrane
Accepting sound—gentle nuance
Into the cloud of Being where
An eternal vista falls

INFINITY

A small creature
You lonely planet
What do you dream?

What do you see
In your little world?

What do you dream
And what does infinity mean to you?
Are you not infinity and
Yourself?

REMINISCENCE

I remember a dream
And the life within

An immense wall
And the wall beyond

The dazzling leaves of the Universe
And the antipode

The silent walk, the water
And climbing the mountain

I remember this very dream
And the life within

FUSION

Slipping into light years' shoes
In light years he walks
Striding to touch the seductive wind of quest

To find himself among the lighthouses
Diving into a galactic sea

By a magnetic force, he's drawn
Into the almighty dream
Only on his mother's bosom to fall again

DERANGEMENT

He was awakened by the sound of air
Its scent and shadow covered him
In its touch, he sensed the silence

He arrived in the space
Where peace waived its wings at him
And at an endlessly distant spot
He saw another being

The closer he moved
The farther it seemed still

REVELATION

The elf arrives with winged vigor,
With a secret whiff, it dilutes the air
His radiant body blows away all doubt
His trail inscribes reconciliation

In the elf's blue eyes, the myriad
Skimming from one island to another
A multitude of tiny winged forces
Trail the elf into mystery

MILLENARIUM

From the flowering palms, the doves will fly,
Smelly rays shining from their eyes
With wavy hair covering landscapes
Taming the Wilderness with a song

Seas are blooming
Inspired by siren singing
The blue curtain sings
Enveloped by the flying gardens

THINKER

His vision
Wanders across bottomless space
Through foggy dreams, it flies
With outward speed
He senses the magical movement

His fire
The purpose of the dream hides
And when dust he becomes
Only his echo
The fog will save

THE OTHER SIDE OF SIGHT

A world discovered
On the other side of sight
Is equal to the open sea—
Timeless, immeasurable

Enchanted by the peace
Of seductive mystery
The sign for meaning that eternity offers

The spark
That sends a river from itself
To itself
Is meaning

River of change
Meaning found in movement
Until peace arrives
At the meeting point of the first source

LIGHT BUGS

PEOPLE LIGHT

To merge with mortar
To feel its truth
In the darkness of frescoes

To see how a soul
Of amulets and temples breathes
To pay respect
To the processions of saints and knights

To meet fathers
Under the yew tree on the hill
And observe an ancient valley
That you are leaving behind

LIGHTHOUSE

Lighthouse in the deep
Lonely Island in the Dark

Every spirit is of the same origin
We all live in the same House

I am in your house, and you are in mine
Everything and nothing in One

Your shining scent arrives
As an invisible orbit to light the way

Recognized only in reverie
Your spirit glows from every spirit

You record every step and every clue
With bright letters that write themselves

Every ray opens a new window
On the big House which glows in the dark

ETHER-PLANE

If I recreate the past—
A lantern above the abyss
Shall I see myself

Shall I sense the condensed ray
When fog begins to shine?
Shall I sit in the ether-plane
When I am taken by suspicion

In an endless vacuum merely
Listening to the sound of fallen times
Before me?
          Cosmos-Vila
          Cosmiliya
Surfaces

A road divided
On which I travel
The land that I long for

MONTENEGRO

Carved out by tectonic folds
It surfaced from the rosy Adriatic Sea
Powerful Lovćen—a friend of storms
The entire mountain—the poet's grave
Twisted landscapes
On two waters
Birds of Vranjina and vegetation of Skadar
Sun in the Sea
Sea in the Sun
People in the Sea and the Sun
Bathe and multiply

Black Mountain—fire bearer
In all sunrises and sunsets

GIANTS

Winter giants came from darkness
To illuminate clearings
Through hidden passages
Descending from the heights

With the melting snow
Into life they rushed
Washed with the glitter
Of wakening dreams

Led by a secret hand
A heavenly smile
A sturdy look
Life was given to them
Short but deep

With snow falling into darkness
Deep snow wants them back

PROTECTIVE WORD

The word and its enticing whistle
Is the internal vision
Of the fire bearer
Coming of age

The word sent to other nests
Peace bearer—world giver

Spark in the eye—lightening
Generous thunder—the word was
Fire borne—a catharsis

HEGEMONIKON

Aristotle's descendant
Staggers in the mud

Thousands of years—
A blinding bright spark of time
Magnificent science transformed
Into fog

One leaf
Blessed peripatetics
Lulled by the eternal dream

There is nobody to wake up eternal seekers
Only a shadow leaks through the present wall
To cover the old leaf in the wind

A CONVERSATION WITH ATOMS

CONVERSATIONS OF ATOMS

In darkness before time
I look at the blossoming of flowers
In the awakening of mist,
Listen to the conversation of atoms

Holly nucleuses
Born and serene
Send offspring toward themselves
The farther away, the closer
The home becomes.

Never lost in wandering
Or consumed by wanderlust

THE FIRST COSMIC DAY

In the cradle of darkness
The incoming glow flickers,
Curdling into clouds
The first dawning scent

Drenched by intoxicating juices
Uninterrupted silent noise
Gets ready for an ultimate breakthrough

The essence of flint strikes,
Giving birth to the day

PATHS

Paths are long and
In limitless ways
Cross-pollinated

Wandering through deserts
To the spring
Deep in which the world bathed
Before its birth

SPRING MUSIC

I can see myself before myself
A being through dark scenery
In foggy surroundings a mere inkling
Lucent and the open space of a dream

Shining light foreboding
Onto frozen space, the light I shed
Into the day as by dream I swim
To the music of nourished meaning

BLOOMING

Memory revived from stone
Imprinted message

The world contained in a seed
Determined by its program

A gleam from a blazing nature
A message written long ago

LITTLE WORLD

A little world finds itself in a bigger
And bigger and bigger and becomes
Dispersed into multitudes
With invisible law

Reflection of the bigger
Seen within itself
Whirl-winding
To draw a distance from itself
And to the one within

By speed, it secures space
There is a pledge of the Big
And of the Small
In the Infinite

WHAT ARE YOU

You are not what you are
You are darkness
Looking for light within
Flying over the untranslatable place
To escape the current whistle
Destruction of the bridge
The place of separation
And move into the foggy glow
To awaken yourself and grow

AWAKENING OF A FLOWER

In nature, nothing is unnatural
Nothing beyond the natural
There are no clear borders
Only merging invisible to the sight

Life into death—
Life's other shape
No rupture
Only crossing

Some mistakes are remainders
Of the hellish awakening of the flower
The roar of the deep

Invisible waves
Hide and pass the message
Across the open abyss
With only an inkling
Where the message comes from

THE CIRCLE

You are hurrying to the sweet place
To the nonsense chasing your spirit
And in the nonsense you look for answers

How far the balance spreads
Where is the limit of sight?

Tiny being,
Into the quest you go
Submerged by persistence
You discover the simplicity of truth
The knot stronger than reality
Preserving the essence

Only one partially submerged reality
In the essence of clearing out and returning
To the end
Of the eternal change gleams,
Is ascended

Through traps set by cowardly peace-keeper
Lured by infinity
You take it on yourself
To tear up the mixed threads

No spring
No sinking
Only bright uniting light

A GRAIN

LONELINESS

Darkness
You were not there

The darkness was longing for you
You, however, for the darkness
And you started shining

THE OPEN DOOR

Nobody enters
Nobody sees the passage
Nobody recognizes the sign

The world is always open
Waiting to be discovered

SUNS AND THE NIGHT

Can nights see the suns
Being born and levitating
Do they take notice of a traveling day

Will the day tell its secret
Before it disappears,
Becomes timeless night

THE STAR AND THE EYE

A dying star is happy
It brightens
Sending its sparkle and a good sleep wish
To itself

When the star dies, its eye closes
Tired of watching,
It flies back to its first bright dream

A GRAIN

Fire sprouts from a grain
The world from fire

Then, water begins to gush
The world to thunder

In the end
The world returns to a grain

A WARDEN WITH NO KEYS

APPROACHING A CLIFF

He awaits himself while walking
Out of the icy circle to escape

On a deserted plain
The wind wildly blows
The tall grass bends over
And he bends himself

There, where he is
Suspecting serenity
In gray surroundings
The game is played

At the very edge
He wakes up
Escaping his fall

ASCENT OF A BARBARIAN

There is enough fire in him to conquer the void
Enough energy to fertilize space
Forces converge and spar within him
Clouds pass through his eyes

He is a destroyer of darkness
An exploding mind that illuminates the sky
A pre-cosmic Big Bang Supernova
Fed by an invisible Quasar

He is a conqueror who creates space
To be able to breathe,
Swinging a chandelier of stars
To fill his night with meaning

When he gets tired, he contracts
The waved Sky returns to where it came from
Noble and silent, rich and wise
Gray-haired, He returns to himself

Only his hair yet illuminates
The edges of galactic roads
His children are still fertile
But his barbarity has disappeared

Now alone—
Biologically spent cosmic aquarium
A clock of fish still bathes within him
But he is leaving

He knows he will be born again
And start fresh anew

ALEXANDER THE GREAT

When the magic of nerves and reason passes
Imagination, force, and passion thunder
The portrait of the world is changed

YAN PALAH

So soon
Palah is dust
The bird that longed for flying

In his longing
For a flight of others
Himself—he handed the torch

Vaclav arranged,
Ready to accept
The live monument

Memory flees
Oblivion erases
And Vaclav's Square reclines in peace

THE BLUE

Feet do engrave the existence of time
On the streets of the cursed
  Blue City

The wavy roar lifts his silhouette
The light leads his sight into the deep
  Blue Sea

His spirit wanders in the heights
The wind blows his breath
Wounded by the beauty of the
  Blue sky

Illuminated by the gentle firmament
He falls into a dream, nourished by the
  Blue sorrow

From one sky into another sky he falls
Stars light up before him, giving birth to the
  Blue death

A MAN AND A MOUNTAIN

He places his arm around the mountain
And they listen to each other

He peeks in the stomach of the mountain
And sees himself

Using the mountain's peak, he cuts
A piece of soft sky for food

Nurtured by the naked horizon
The man and the mountain are cursed
To merge the roots

SHAMAN IN THE BLUE MOUNTAIN

With its hills, the mountain defies heights
With massive, levitating rocks
It can hide its prenatal spirit

Shaman feels the cold power of years
In the jump through the history of intricate layers
He tames furious forces

The pulsating mountain
Gives in to a Shaman and
Speaks to him
And the Shaman gives in to the mountain
And receives her strength

IN THE SILENCE OF THE CENTURY

Feel the force of
Morning freshness
Ticklish scents

You last in the moment
Do not lose your sensibility
Your only existence
Pierces holes in the sky
Peeking through thin heights

Give in to the silence
The coldness of centuries
Pass through the tree
To the source
Accept the light and wait

To jump over centuries
In one step is impossible
Jump too high or far,
You'll be way too late

THE CALL

A white bird flies out
From a dark sea
Followed by myriad flocks that
Spread fresh sweetness from the source

Big shining waves
Flood the blue firmament
With an enchanting song
They spread the merging charm

Birds' soft touches
Offer a smelly heaven
A powerful force is asking for
The beauty of the moment

The night is still waiting

IN SEARCH OF SPARK

A hidden spark of the dream sleeps
In the forest and waits
In the celestial spheres of the brain

Little eyes watch from the forest
The mixed traces of spirit
Hurrying to meet itself
To light the light of epiphany

THE SAME DUST

You cannot escape
You are deceived
An illusion floats around you
Casting spells, tripping you

Tripping is better perhaps
Than to disappear too early

All dust is the same dust
Temporarily separated
To go peacefully
And enjoy the eternal nap

THE THIN THREAD

Forces crush each other
Dust is your beginning
The fall—your truth

You dance on a thin thread
It is a sad move
To outlive yourself
To prove improvably

To the knights of faith that
Nobody believes

NEW VANDALS

New vandals will destroy New Rome
God always remains silent

New vandals will destroy
What the old ones forgot to abolish

If people have a voice
It would be good for them to fight

If they stay silent, it will be too late
Vandals listen only when others are weaker

If they are equal or stronger
Their word is the last word

Deliver thunder, God
If you choose not to talk

DARKNESS IS WAITING

FIGHT

The bird is the freedom lover
Hunters kill it

The tree defies the sky
Head cutters deface it

The earth is life giver
Conquerors cover it

The grass, the flowers
A Noble Nature

Steel, plastic, noble metals
Who will swallow what?

All swallows all
Life must eat life to survive

THE TREES OF STONE

From the primordial sea-void
The trees of stone grow

Round stony worlds on treetops sleep
Waiting for their moment to shine

Tight and crystal rings
On the wavy base of a snowy sea

People walk to the other shore
Over the icy landscape

Circling galactic ways
Reflected in the sky

To the murmur of time immemorial
Trees listen and spread their roots wider

Into the cosmic abyss, treetops fly
Fed only by light and music beyond the scale

LIGHTENING THE ABYSS

The Sun's girandole from East
To West ponders as the light parade falls

Furious winds chased by Aeolus
Confused people—staggering propellers

Dusty tornado confuses man's senses.
He cannot recognize the crazy game

BEAST

Beast in the eye
From the eye the tooth grows
Exterminator
Against exterminator

Jammed into a spasm
Two huge bodies stall
Move neither forward
Nor backward

Neither alive nor dead
No one lets up
No one wins

ANIMALIZATION

He gazes into emptiness
Long—it lasts long
The hair grows long
Killing rays he sees abound
He escapes into the forest of emotions
Wakening extinguished instincts.
He has no faith
When he recognizes the danger
He is ready to jump
Roaring in the beginning
To scare
And if needed, he jumps high
Landing on all fours
With a piece of human flash
In his teeth

SPACES OF PEACE

Hungry shackles stand
On the deserted shore
Ugly and mute

Looking for the flowery fields
The place of peace
Lost long ago
When the shackles thought
They were human

VISION

What kind of words are these?
Known letters,
But unknown meanings

What kind of picture,
Carried from outer space is this?
What kind of vision
Or is it only a dream
Carried from outer space

People hanged
Skeletons
Processions of tortured
Who forgot the glamour and the arrogance
Modestly moved into voluntary caves
So keen to continue
Into uncertainty

THE CHESSBOARD

Dusty ground draws the map
Of misfortunes that are waiting
Even cactus is thinning
Being transformed
Into a threatening thorn

On a faraway chessboard
Nobody makes moves
Only an endless hot peace prevails

Children crawl
Together with others
In the animal kingdom
Fighting to survive
They eat the future children

ARRIVAL OF DARKNESS

Awakened eternity
Flows down from the sky
By a sparkly drapery
Of black waves

The oldest color
Soaks up the soft serenity
The curtain falls to hide the stage

RIVER OF DEATH

Cosmic sirens ring
From sky cliffs as
The River of Death flows
Digging into Earth's arteries
Boils and splashes
Mixes muck and flower
Sucked away by hellish water
Thirsty, furious as though
Panting agony of gods
Breaking sky,
In the fusion and fission of atoms,
Grubs up the root of the Universe
Putrefying all existence

The Earth's stomach
Awakens skeletons that rush out
Skulls that moan
Merged in huge balls
Flocks of orphaned eyes fly
Furies invigorate all fogs
Eyesight leaks into the fiery pot
Arrows lie silent
Sharpness broken, dulled once again
The shredded circle cries in the mud
Of forgotten calamity
The truth shines and emerges
Lightening from the mighty blue light
Smashes the remnants

Unexplainable peace, then
Suddenly, a thunder
Delivers a final blow, and
Death swallows itself

A MELODY OF THE PRIMEVAL HOME

When you fly away
To a vacuum with no gravity
Where all forces negate one another
And melt into an overpowering dream

When you sense the call
Of ancient vistas
Picture a place where
Solitude is a protective blanket

When in the full lap
Of the eternal Mother you fall asleep
The melody of the primordial home
Will lull you

Until the next reawakening
In who knows what form
But you will wait

A WORD

A word only writes
Its night and rides
Its dream

ABOUT THE AUTHOR

Dejan Stojanović was born in Peć in 1959. He graduated from the Law School of the University of Priština. He has published books of poems:
The Sun Observes Itself (Sunce sebe gleda), NIP Književna reč, Belgrade, 1999.
The Sign and Its Children (Znak i njegova deca), Prosveta, Belgrade, 2000.
The Creator (Tvoritelj), Narodna knjiga, Belgrade, 2000.
The Shape (Oblik), Gramatik, Podgorica, 2000.
The Dance of Time (Ples vremena), Konras, Belgrade, 2007.

Pentalogy: *The World in Nowherness (Svet u nigdini):*
1. *Ozar (Ozar),* Udruženje književnika Srbije, Belgrade, 2017.
2. *The World and God (Svet i Bog),* Udruženje književnika Srbije, Belgrade, 2017.
3. *The World in Nowhereness (Svet u nigdini),* Udruženje književnika Srbije, 2017.
4. *The World and Humans (Svet i ljudi),* Udruženje književnika Srbije, Belgrade, 2017.
5. *The Home of Light (Dom svetlosti).* Udruženje književnika Srbije, Belgrade, 2017.

The Hidden Light (Skrivena svetlost), Čigoja, Belgrade, 2018.
Primordial Spark (Iskra iskona), Albatros plus, Belgrade, 2021.
Centuries and Steps (Vekovi i koraci), Albatros plus, Belgrade, 2023.

Essays:
Creator and Creating (Stvaralac i stvaranje), Albatros plus, Belgrade, 2021.
The New Man and the New World (Novočovek i novosvet), Rad, Belgrade, 2022.

Anthology: *Selected Serbian Plays* (*Izabrane srpske drame*), USA, 2016.

Philosophy: *Absolute*, New Avenue Books, USA, 2024.

A book of his selected interviews, Conversations, was published in 1999 by NIP Književna reč, Belgrade. The Serbian Heritage Foundation and the Association of Writers of Serbia for Intellectual Engagement awarded the book the Rastko Petrović Prize.

www.ingramcontent.com/pod-product-compliance
Lightning Source LLC
Chambersburg PA
CBHW020548130626
46552CB00007B/2815